Emma Strunk

Tony Nesca

By Tony Nesca

Stale Anchovy Kisses -

Dead Bats Amidst The Bullshit Laughter And The Lovestricken Cockroaches –

Hollow Man –

La Gioconda -

Charlie -

Mondo Cane -

Dishpig -

About A Girl -

Emma Strunk -

Jukebox Music -

La Gioconda (the novel) -

The Do-Nothing Boys -

Bulletproof Smile -

Vodka Orange Sunday -

Hobo –

Crazy Legs –

Junkyard Lucy -

Last Stop To Saskatoon -

Emma Strunk Copyright © 2005 Tony Nesca

ISBN - 978-1-7752112-5-9

Published by Screamin' Skull Press

screamingskullpress.net/

Printed in the U.S.A.

**What you are about to read is a
work of fiction**

EMMA STRUNK

NEON CRAZY

guy called timmy sits alone

drink in hand

says rock and roll is dead

friend bob collects welfare thinks

girlfriend called tracy wants nothing chain-

smoking du mauriers

the occasional heroin hit

timmy says it's not real pours a whiskey for me

i think about murder or suicide but not really

bob wears a bandanna, runs with the gangs

tracy reads the tao feeling purple

and crazy,

outside the snow falls across the rooftops of peg

zero

no one knows

no one sings

no one cries like we should,

a filthy apartment in the wind,

a shitty lover under the sun,

timmy don't want rays of light

he want electric guitar and

the genius in the crowd,

tracy giving all she can,

bob screaming at the welfare clerk,

no one cries like they should...

DIAMONDS IN HIS EYES

reggie sitting here

not saying much

mike plays the piano talking

'bout kurt cobain

diamonds in his eyes

he didn't want fame

he says

didn't want it

reggie's awake eyes of

rock smoke twirls

to the ceiling

blue lights flashing

mike laughing wild

not really wanting it

he says

not really like

money and flatulence and

alone moments at the bus-stop

he's got an aunt in wisconsin

one in halifax
they singing canadian
songs drinking wine
and moosehead beer
they're not really here
he says
not really
mike's got the powder
demon inside him
his sister paints tattoos
on the arms of the
lonely
yeah
eyes of the lonely
jukebox in the corner
a spike inside his brain
everything's alright
they be smiling in
the night under
the neon
the caramba
in the ocean 'round

a room covered in mambo

hallucinations

hey hey

indigo

mike he's crying

doesn't really want to

not really

thinking music is a

wonderful illness

time for more

time for another

reggie laughs

no more barroom isolation

a knock on the door

"who is it?" says mike

"yeah!" says reggie,

"it's emma" says a voice,

the world crumbles and

i begin to think...

A COUPLE GIRLS THEY START TALKING

they stand in line it's –30
waiting for the band and the gorilla
at the front to let them
through they smoking hash
out of a carrot
reggie he smiling
mike's wondering what happened to his girl
reggie don't care about girls
or cars and rock and roll
his groove is central park
the dark here and now
of main street
a couple of girls they start talking
mike's dreaming reggie does his
street dance the girls diggin' this
beautiful black thing,
ooooohhh they say

owwieeee

yahooooooo

reggie glides across the snow

bumps into timmy

they smile and move on

the streetlights flash orange

"mike" says reggie

"mike"

his girl is in his head

in his guts

up his ass

on the street

in the bouncer's eyes

she's in his hands

in his pockets

in the reflection of the night

she's crawling up his leg

she's chewing on his brain,

it's like that sometimes...

GHETTO BITCH

at the corner store tracy

looking for a fix

bob's a raunchy motherfucker

knocked her front teeth out

insists he loves her

she says he's the cat's ass

in summer he walks around bare

chest flabby tits while tracy

looks lost forced smile

not really knowing much

but funny girl she's 4'8"

talks with a tiny lisp likes to

help people

bought me a hot-dog once

sold me some grass

never sucked my cock but

that's cool

"hey bob" i say

"buddy, you looking for smoke?"

"don't got the dough man."
"let's smoke a joint."
"where's tracy?"
"lost in her own fucking head."
"you think maybe you got something to do with
that?"
"what the fuck you saying?"
"hey, let's smoke that joint."
"no really, what the fuck you mean?"
he pauses trying to look scary then lights up
then we're laughing,
there's tracy across central park
looks like a midget she's talking
to mike reggie's groovin'
in rhythm hot hot
sun scorching the grass
my brain feels stoned and on fire
tracy's with us bob kisses her
"seen anyone?" she says
no one answers
kids are shooting hoops
a couple of drunks pass a bottle

a cabby sits on a bench motor running

mike smiles gives me a handshake

"i saw emma" I say...

everyone shakes as the cold runs down our

spine.....

SCREAM

grew up in the barbados they called him

reggie came to peg zero smoking

ziggy's cigar like all the rest

ending up in the core area

he be cruising the streets

with pirate sensibilities lives

at a whorehouse surrounded by

tits and ass all funky pearls

now it's true he's a junky

it's true he's a hustler

it's also true he doesn't give a shit about me or

you

got beat up the other day

saw the violence on his face

reggie i said

owed some green he said

smiled that sad smile

"why you stay here?" i said

"nowhere else" he said

nowhere place
nowhere nothing zero in peg zero
who you think you fuckin' with?
shake his hand and move on
timmy walks by with bob too much
snow i'm thinkin',
they're smoking cigs. and
frowning in the dusk
"were you here for the fire?" says timmy
reggie's on the corner
he thinkin'
he movin'
there's a whore with him wearing
black boots reaching for the sun
three headed lobster boy thighs
in my mind she reaches for her purse
she got long black curls tickling her ass
i see mike he's stumbling leaning
against the wind,
time to talk
and laugh
and maybe

just maybe

move on from here...

LAURA IN A PURPLE DRESS

long black hair white face
vampire bites tattooed on
her neck she got army
boots long purple dress
yeah it's the cool and the crazy
it's the dave wisdom show
as tough as nails
as blinding as snow on
a sunny day in peg zero
when the sun goes down
she talks about no rent
no food a day like
any other in the core
area of peg zero
mike's her man
he drinks she don't like
it, i drink she says

nothing,
laura is her name as
stunning as orange phoenix
"my mother hates me" she says,
then she cries
i hug her not knowing
what else to do
it's midnight the dogs are
out,
there's a fire across the street,
sirens invade my room
i have a rye and 7 in hand
dreaming of the congo
of venice and of
happier times in peg zero
in the silence of my dreams
hitchhiking 'cross the land
trying to make it work
trying not to laugh
in my dreams
bartender gives me a wink,
a double scotch and

a smile.............

LOST IN THE LAUGHTER

at mike's place,
laura's here and reggie
and timmy we're waiting
for tracy to deliver
the goods all drinking,
laughing, a knock at the door
tall black chick walks
in she's a hooker says mike
hey have a drink i say,
she has some wine
scar on her cheek says
joe-blow knifed her
she talking about her kids
in toronto it's all crimson-sad
but mike's laughing
it's friday night
the criminals are out
we want nothing to do with
the rest,

tracy arrives pulls out

the rock, i decline as usual

they're into it

i'm smoking pot and the booze

feels like the beginning

of something good,

the hooker keeps suggesting

i'm a narc

laughable of course

cops are idiots and

i'm stupid but

my brand of stupidity

is better than yours

yeah,

better than yours,

laura freaking out

mike takes it cool and sensitive

reggie's got some kind of internal drama

tracy you beautiful midget

the hooker's lost in the laughter

i seem to be an island of calm

in the midst of this natural

bullshit

"hey you" says timmy.

"yeah?" i say.

"drinking is no good, no damn good."

he's drunk while he says it

so i forgive him

tiny room in a ghetto high-rise

ain't so pretty hooker asks

to use my phone we exit down

the hall into my apartment

she's on the phone long slit flashing

thigh and hip,

i want her,

i want her so badly my cock

is screaming in chinese

dirty hallway this whore's six feet

of lost beauty she towers over

me…

…and her in the pacific,

we're at mike's

laura's screaming

her obvious power annoying

as dandelions

mike gentle and kind

madness whiskey revival

only i can satisfy this reality

i'm a carpenter in jerusalem

i'm a painter in saskatoon

i'm a rapist in waikiki

my name is ziggy

and peg zero is my dream....

THE FIRE

turns out mike

was lighting the pipe

when the alarm went off

there was pam down the hall

all coked-up

simone the stripper

and her little boy bobby

bobby he screaming

FIRE FIRE

reggie hangin'

at mike's laura looking

dark and wanton

timmy on the 12th floor

smoking grass he be smiling

there ain't no fire he says

i ignore the alarm

have a beer and a toke

i got angel city on the

ghetto

there ain't no fire i say

doors open people be running

up and down the hall

full of smoke down the stairwell

it's a madhouse i'm stumbling

down 18 floors getting stronger

each landing a bum

squats he be sniffin'

turpentine

there's timmy screaming

some shit, hey there's ricardo

the drug dealer

smiling like a snake

in sicily

an otter in quebec

a hockey player in brazil

on the 8th floor is the

most smoke t-shirt over mouth, tired legs

screamin', old people and kids they be crying,

kids they be painful, lobby crowded we're in

the convenience store through the hallway, full

crowd here, storekeeper asks me to keep an eye

on the thieves, they're shoving chips and colas

down their shirts, it's free game, free living,

bob he's selling to some punks it's

fucking freezing outside

firefighters everywhere city brings

in the buses we're getting

warm huddled together all losing

bastards

lobby crowded

store crowded

buses crowded

mike spots me waving a joint

he's outside i join him

laura comes around then bob

and tracy we're passing the spleef

i spot emma in the crowd

i tell the others

she disappears wait says bob,

there she is, he looks terrified,

we look

a hint of brown curls

then nothing...to do

waiting around mike has container

of vodka and orange

we're drinking in the cold

cold peg zero night

moon invisible

brain too tiny to mention

breath coming out in clouds

above above a sky full

of laughing and mocking

be brave

be thinking

vodka almost gone

get the word

no elevators 'till morning

we begin the trek hoses and sprinklers 500

of us getting soaked

stair after stair legs

a nightmare can't be happening i think

lungs full of shit i laugh

with mike frowning laughing

frowning laura pissed as

always

tracy that crazy tiny tiny
woman running the stairs
like an acrobat she flying
past me
old lady sitting water pouring down her
back, can't make it she's saying,
can't make it,
i take her arm
mike takes other
burden in tow we proceed
where's emma now?
where she at that screaming beauty
old lady breathing like she's
dying i'm encouraging her
it's okay
mike stops at 11th floor
along with bob and tracy
laura too
they're jonesin' for the next hit
bum with matted hair crumbles
we're on the 14th old lady says
she lives on the 21st while

jesus and buddha have a beer at the winnipeg
hotel
down broadway and at a cafe on montmartre
laugh you ancient buggers, life is for the young
shoes full of water, hair like bob marley, old
lady down to her knees, then up around my
arm, i slip on the water, she grabs my shirt, we
continue past 18 tempting me to curse her hide,
we reach the 21st,
she hangs on dearly, i'm laughing, i'm lighting
a smoke, mike bob tracy laura on their second
rock,
on montmartre
down via roma, times square
the hills of vienna
old lady at home maybe dying
i crash on the couch
wet clothes, hair like charley manson,
legs finished lungs
deflated
i waver in and out
darkness confusing sights

feeling death on my shoulder

vision regained

slowly lungs open up

legs cramped but ok.,

i struggle to a glass of beer

wet body stain on couch i light a joint

start feeling

alive

mike arguing with laura

reggie grooving against the world

the phone rings

sun starts to shine

i've had 6 joints 12 beers and 29 cigarettes

i feel the need to continue

look around

water trail up and down

phone rings again i pause

uncertain

undetermined

guilty

a knock on my door...

I LOVE YOU SHE SAYS

living mad living crazy laura's
always at my door,
"can i use the phone" she says,
does it ten times a day
trying to score that
latest sensation expecting
something different
same old shit happens
she's broke, can't afford phone,
her and mike
slip grass under my door
wrapped in nice tiny
packages penciled by laura
crayon drawings of vampires
killers hangmen and
axe-slingers laura she's screaming now
tired of this life she says
mike takes it as always
he too sensitive and kind

works on a forklift everyday

drinks every night

apartment is tiny 3 big televisions

goth icons

mike he fucks up, no lie there

he's late on rent

late on bills

always on time for happy hour

he lights a smoke now while laura

shouts and slams her fist

they get some rock later

things settle down he hugs her

she moans, says i love you, don't ever leave

me...

mike he's got tears in his eyes

a beautiful evening

the sun sets...

mike works

laura watches soaps, smokes grass

she's at my place on the horn

she's begging for money

she's screaming fuck this, fuck that,

mike is back home the fighting begins

then they cuddle like monkeys

i love you she says

i love you he says

i open a fresh pack of smokes, light a joint, turn

the t.v. on

but it don't mean shit...

A NIGHT WITH REGGIE

reggie lives at a whorehouse
small place, bad seed, nice ladies
they walk about hardly dressed
his job is to keep an eye open
which he does one called destiny
tall native woman long black spirals
we drink at a place on kennedy drive,
"my father was jamaican, you know?" she says
"yeah" i say "oh yeah."

so she with reggie this night at the
hooker-shack usual bullshit
going in and out
other ladies doing fine
smoking cigarettes madame
too young insists no drugs while
working reggie he lights up
destiny takes a puff,
"reggie" she says

he smiles,
"reggie, reggie."
he looks out window
sees sirens and desperation
thinks about barbados then destiny
she's bouncing on his shoulders
reggie in lovely pain
ah-huh he's saying, uh-huh
she puts a smoke in his mouth
bounces down, down
thighs around head
ass on shoulders he doing fine
she drags him from room to room
screams down the hallway, smoke in the
mirror,
reggie's just fine man
just fine......

DESTINY

3 kids, boyfriend a gang member,

i used to work as a security guard at high-rise

across the street

destiny's boyfriend came in every night

with gang buddies tough boys

drunk and screaming

two-fisted howling

he was good to me

saved my ass once

in high-rise across the street

tough place, things gone wiry

destiny...

three kids demanding

gang boyfriend

rumors are he killed a man

destiny sad and tough

beautiful woman could be model or actress

but it's peg zero

hills of malibu unattainable

whorehouse down the street

she lives it well

can never destroy her

from manitoba indian reserve

tough living no stranger

baby in arms he begging

picks her son up from school

chats with other parents feeling

superior

sucking cock at night

dodging bullets under the sun

she smiles and freezes the world,

and it's all there,

just for her,

a pause, a frown and a cup of tea,

time for work

thinking about reggie and that caribbean smile

the john with the hairy gut

the girls proud and sad

some are junkies

some mothers and wives

all as right as anything

she laces her leather boots

it's raining outside

inside warm and blue

door slams open gang boyfriend

comes in blood on face

something dark in hand, fuzzy

not clear,

then he screams............

she thinks about a small child

on a waterfall,

on a lake,

in the woods in her

grandmother's arms,

a sweaty old man between her legs,

it's everywhere, she says, everywhere...

BOB CRIES

hangin' with destiny on sargent and langside

she's gotta go

i think of this girl i knew

in italy as an adolescent

destiny's thighs keep moving

i keep dreaming, it's winter

cold as love in a heartbeat

wanting destiny not having destiny

same thing in the snow on a rise

by a river or

a skyscraper......

black guy i know with dreads

in the neighborhood

hooked on pills

white guy hooked as well

i light a joint

i'm a white man from italy

pale-faced

light eyes

light hair

bob is sitting in front of the toob

tracy trying to laugh

the crack is out

bob slaps her hard

they argue about something entirely

irrelevant

tracy says she's had enough

enough

enough of the shit

the macho resolutions

"you're a prick!"

another act of violence this time

it's a clenched fist

tracy reels all 4'8" of her

but she laughs

laughs

this is what breaks bob's heart...

i'm at home as this happens

no money or anything

i'm drunk or stoned

not feeling right

not liking men with their violence

not liking women with their desire

a cool head in the maelstrom

i think

i suppose

maybe i'm wrong, for the first

and last time

i consider this...

bob is crying

tracy is tasting her blood

i feel laughter in my heart

but i don't believe it...

IL VIGLIACCO

"i'll tell ya this story" I say…

"yeah?" she says…

"i used to live

in italy,

my uncle

took me to

soccer games,

torino was my team,

my cousins

always with me,

70,000 people in

an outdoor

stadium,

screaming,

fighting,

cloudy sky,

banners on every

curve,

banners up my

ass,

just outside

a long street

lined

with

newsstands

fat guy

serving cappuccino,

porn mags,

cigarettes,

down the street

was La Fiat

industrial gray

car manufacturer,

gypsies everywhere man,

they begging

and scamming,

trumpets

screaming,

I'm going

deaf

with

violence,

exaggerated passions,

uncle shouting

crazy,

cousins fat

and

lazy,

girl with pigtails

short skirt,

i'm distracted but

the rest

don't

give

a

shit,

game slow,

maddening with

inactivity,

i'm insane

I said"…

"yeah?" she says...

"yeah, end of
game,
our team
loses,
bullshit
erupts,
there
be
violence
in
the
stands,
rival fans clashing,
riot squad
with
tear
gas we're stuck
up top,
guy

with

switchblade

he

screaming, "hey blondie, if I see ya

downtown.."

waving blade

all ridiculous,

all beautiful,

all

insane

laughter,

later on boulevard rabid fan

rips flag out

of

my

hands,

i'm an adolescent

but

i'm angry

at that

big italian

prick…"

"well, you must be a very proud
young man to tell stories like that..." she says
moving
towards
me...

"i'll tell ya what i think..." she smiles,
we square off and it begins again...

WASTED DAY AT THE WHOREHOUSE

destiny she whistles through her
teeth when you're stoned it's
freaky cuz you don't know
where it's coming from
she sitting there smiling
the wind blowing through
your ears
reggie throws the ace
"damn you" says destiny,
"damn you!...hear about trent?"

"trent?" says reggie...

"he was shanked by the river..."

"no shit?"

"no shit, and i think bob's next",
she slams the 7 on the table
takes a shot of brandy
reggie he cool counteracts with
the three of diamonds...

"you're fucked" she says...

the whores gliding by
precise as water
doors slamming
ulcers bursting
madam may i genuflect
"hot in here" says reggie,
"up yours" says destiny slamming
the ace of spades
the ace of spades
goddamn, a joint is lit
"bob was shot when he was a teen" says
reggie...

"yeah?"

"clear through the chest from the back,
it was an accident me thinkin'..."

"nothing can kill that mother,
i hear he beats tracy..."

"that motherfucker beats on that midget?"

"she ain't no midget, just
a tiny sad woman..."

whore stops and talks to destiny
she don't want this particular john,
"he vile" she says...
"if he pays you spread" says destiny
"you spread bitch",
reggie hurls the 4 of clubs
"not nothing no way anyhow"
says destiny with a wave of the hand
outside hot and raining
everyone sweating

everyone dancing
sun go down game continue,
"mike owes me a rock" says reggie
barbados too distant
destiny whistles thinks
of her kids at school,
wooden desks
cardboard teachers
whore waving stinkin' ass
reggie blasted
destiny drunk stars in eyes
"did you hear about laura?" she says...

that very second laura's
at home
watching soaps,
smoking rock,
she ain't thinking shit,
she doing the crack waltz
spinning round and round
down and under
under

under...

IT SHAKES HER BOOTS

mike sensitive guy timmy's there too

mike says laura's a dominatrix

likes to use him as a chair,

timmy he thinking and smoking

thinking and smoking,

but she's gained weight lately

should i tell her?

timmy don't give a hoot

cuz he likes plato and so-crates

mike paper-thin ribs like

rice paper

there's an ill wind blowing

through central park

through the core area of

peg zero

the junkies feel it

the trendies and the hoods

the drunken writers

the lonely painters

the immigrant families

lonely happy completely mad

infected with living

emma feels it too

stilettos clicking through urban

landscape in and out of shadows

up fire escapes

down the cobblestone

past the dealers and the yuppies

a hotdog stand quivers

street artists earn their keep

as the wind whistles softly

past emma's heels up her

leather skirt

it knots her ties

it shakes her boots

her wild curls scream in mandarin

the abstract truth like

a spike in her veins

timmy smiles at mike

mike's not digging it

two months behind in the rent

phone disconnected

abstract truth slicing through

your brain...

HANGIN' AT BOB AND TRACY'S

so i says to him,
"he hung himself right in that same room we
used to"-
"-lend me a ten" says bob...
"sure" i say
tracy seems to be smiling
despite that crazy bob ex-con
ex-pimp
ex-human
he gives me a beer for
this i love him
tracy talks to her kids on the phone
she crying and laughing
crying and laughing
once again bob lights the rock
smoke makes a direct line to his brain
he's not scary considering

quite funny actually

wouldn't want to piss him off

so i do just that,

"what the fuck you mean?" he says,

"hey", i say "hey, easy," he gives me another

beer

says i'm a good guy

walks out of the room

tracy off the phone

telling me bob's a dangerous

dangerous man

she scared

she trapped

emma fixed him good once she says

that mandarin beauty

that viking terror

dark eyes long arms

"tracy get the fuck out of this" i say,

no response in the frozen winter

of peg zero dirty apartment

stranded in the snow

and ice and prairie isolation

-35 outside says tracy

sisters of mercy on blaster

reggie walking the streets

mike huddled in darkness

"couldn't find a job if i wanted one" she says,

"you don't want one" i say,

"no, things are shitty"

bob's back laughing lost and vicious

gentle with me calls tracy a bitch

tracy lights the pipe complaining

about absence of kids

takes another puff,

"i miss them",

another puff,

"i miss them",

volunteers at sally-ann on week-end

"i went to sally-ann once" i say "didn't really

need to,

just curious",

"you took a meal", she says, puff puff,

"took a meal from someone who needs it",

they offer me the pipe

i turn it down
bob and tracy looking at me like i'm missing
brain matter
"keep powder family away from me" i say,
then i take another beer
feeling typical and unoriginal
disoriented and unoriginal
but i write i say
say it like it's something holy
i write...

and i knew a woman called betsy once
and i've seen the mediterrean but
that ain't nothing
gypsy on the corner says tracy, sells
flowers and sucks cock to
support her heroin habit
"that ain't nothing" i say
i leave and take the stairwell
to my place on the 18th
floor
there's a gray film on the walls

stairs dirty blue and wandering

reminding me of something

the vast blue of the med

the smoke curling to the ceiling

the mountains of northern italy

the stone of the canadian shield

in my apartment cd's scattered over the

hardwood

a half-bag of grass and

the lengthy thighs of the whorehouse on the

corner

in every whorehouse

on every corner

reminding me of something

rejection letters from publishers

jobs denied

jobs unwanted

letters never written

reminding me of something

an inflatable in my closet

as i reach for it

it moves further and further and i follow

and i follow the dark stench of
never-mind and never-glory
all around me....

FREUD AND PLATO

that damn timmy sitting around
my place
always getting shitkicked by women
i'm thinkin' he likes it
speaks of freud and plato constantly
yeah, you a smart boy timmy
emma busted his ribs once
he be telling me
he be talking always
and forever
"got a joint?" he says
"see ya later timmy"
he leaves then i light a joint
graceful in his absence i hear
action down the hall
voices, screams
someone demanding money
laura telling the voice fuck you!
it goes on

on

on

i turn the tv down

nothing happening

i listen to tunes

nothing happening

i open a beer

sit at my window

stare at the peg zero skyline

exchange district spreading out

drunken couple fighting

i light a smoke

cop car in the distance

firetruck on its way

laura walks in

she's crying

she got fat lip, blood on forearm

mike back home hurtling at the sky

laura's screaming

there's nothing happening...

TIMMY ONCE AGAIN

mike laura tracy and bob

got some shit going down

owe money to everyone

laura stands in line at food banks

mike works his ass off

bob sells crack

tracy smokes it

i'm the outsider as timmy

runs down an alley

a very large, very beautiful,

very angry native woman

behind him...

ANOTHER FINE MESS

on his way to work mike looks

at the clouds

let it rain he says

down ellice then young street

little boy on doorstep

mike gives him some gum

a pat on the head

keeps moving

6 am.

footsteps in the distance

closer now

workplace visible

rumbles in the dawn

glint on metal

blood on mike's leg and arm

sensitive eyes

tender heart wounded

and shattered

he sits in own blood

uncaring sky above
destiny standing on corner
end of shift
she kneeling beside him
long curls flowing
thighs of magic
breasts like atom bombs
mike smiles...

three days later reggie
talking about barbados
mike's passing a joint with
bandaged arm
i take it laura gone for
the night
much quieter without her
mike laughing loud without her
4 am.
mike leaves for more
of the insanity
reggie he waiting and nervous
looks out window mike in

central park accosted by

shadow

"me thinkin'" says reggie "this no good"

smoke pours out of my mouth

beautiful curls of blue

then reggie screaming he running

i'm behind at elevator

we're down in convenience store

rapid speed past the potato chips and the cash

register

and the african fellow behind the counter

we're in the park

large man pounding on mike

moon up above

light rain on shoulders

i'm pulling fucker off

reggie clocks him good, we're with mike

in his apartment

mike breathing heavy sad and lonely

5 am.

dark lost madness

mike attracts this

he navigates random universe
wounded at every turn i grab
a beer
mike looks at me
he too small
his eyes tell me this
they also tell me he's a junky
he's confused
he's not long for this world
hoping i'm horrendously mistaken
i offer him a beer and
a thank you...

A BIT OF HISTORY

laura's father was a junky,
overdosed last year, mother
a drunk...

mike grew up with distant father,
bad side of peg zero,
caught brother fucking laura
one night...

brother now dead...

reggie grew up in the barbados,
rumors he was raped by drunken
uncle under a banana tree...

timmy raised in greece by
schizophrenic mother,
spent summers in venice
came to peg zero and hit

the crack pipe...

my childhood was an early morning
in the grass...

i thank the gods every day...

BOB GETS POPPED

"it's the gray in here" he says,

lighting smoke exhaling

cell buddy grinnin',

"my clothes

the walls

the bars

everything gray..."

he got it good

he supplies the inside with grass

three meals a day

started a wood-working class

spends nights watching the tube

getting high

talking shit and laughing

"this ain't so bad" he says,

"ain't so bad..."

bob he's carving
a small figure of a native
girl this time,
she's wearing moccasins
and smiling,
"if it wasn't for the gray" he says...

native girl she grooving
with the wind
she be pointing wooden fingers
laughing and taunting
he throws it across the room
raging against the machine...

"what's up?" says cellmate

"it's the gray" he says,
"it's all this fucking
gray..."

BOB'S GONE

tracy skipping through central park

it's aboriginal day

celebrations of a great culture

drums pounding

traditional dancers smiling at the sun

tracy she laughing,

she singing with the children

she picking flowers

everything is blue and alive

beautiful and aquamarine

bob's gone

and that much is right

with the world...

BLUES ON THE RADIO

laura,
tears run silently down her
cheeks
coffee in front of her
old blues song on the radio
mom too tired and hungover
laura wanting happiness
wanting understanding
mom too tired and wasted
ain't no purpose she says,
there ain't none
mike at home lighting a
rock
tears on his cheek
heavy metal on the ghetto
no family
friends an illusion
"c'mon," says reggie,
"it ain't so bad"

laura hands mom a cig.

mom shaking the hangover

chills

shaking hand lights a match

laura

looks out window

kids playing in the snow

mailman on corner blows out smoke

a firetruck makes its run,

ain't no purpose she says,

there ain't none

mike shakes reggie's hand

"we're not going to make it, are we?"

reggie smiles

laura cries

"no..." says reggie,

"but who the hell does?"

BLOOD IN THE LOBBY

walk through the convenience store

there's a door through a dark hallway

that leads to the main

lobby and the

elevators

past the bums and the sniffers

the crackheads

the drunks

the potheads

the working-class immigrants

the few trendy university students

scars on the wall

broken bottles on the floor

sometimes blood in the lobby

bob used to hang here selling

rock

now reggie took over

but he too friendly this

barbados refugee

he too kind and crafty

too wasted

chillin'

and

shaky

hands awry, crocodiles too drunk

wolverine in the dark doorway

i look at reggie

i look at our caretaker

old bat hump on back

gimp leg

fears no one this wiry strega

i look at laura

i look at the sun

the moon

the car exhaust

the old man shovelling snow

from the driveway broken down

house nothing but a shack

on corner by whorehouse

all lit up like

a carnival

destiny walks with back straight

emma sticks to the shadows

i look at all this,

shake my head

thinkin',

i got nothing to say man,

nothing....

AFTERNOON IN DODGE CITY

"i'm tired of this", says destiny
i take the joint
put it to my lips
she got long legs
long chin
eyes like the devil
eyes beautiful in love
she crosses her legs
asks me,
"how 'bout you, how are things?"

she got dark native skin
exotic smooth in love
bare legs drive me wild
mad and insane
fingernails red as fire
grandmother up north

on dry reserve crime

and desperation on every corner

we laugh like it's that easy

frozen and immaculate

it's grace and suave luck

it's synchronicity on wheels

god on the corner barstool

i raise a hand,

she crosses her legs

one big thigh over the other

i look up her skirt,

she caresses my face,

we talk

calmly

determined

smiling

a touch of laughter in the air.....

JUST ANOTHER NIGHT TOM WAITS ON THE STEREO

out my window on the 18th floor

view of downtown skyline and

old warehouses of the exchange district

looks like a small chicago

beautiful and terrifying

urban madness

down at street level

hot summer night

some young punks get into

punching clawing beating

with vicious precision

ungrateful at their luck

of having been blessed with

geography

would you rather be in afghanistan?

the violence continues

i call the cops

i scream at the moon

why, i say,

WHY?

there ain't no solution

there can't be

we were wired faulty from the beginning

it's not about toxic emissions

or environmental rape

or serial killers salivating

at the

crotch

or planes slamming into the

world trade centre

or america with its hidden agendas

or canada with its indifference

or europe with its pseudo-sophisticated elitism

or street gangs running the streets

killing like that's all they know,

it's about US,

US,

every last one of us...

i look back down at
the street, the cops are hauling
the punks away
i smile,
there's a knock on my
door,
mike says it's time for a drink
"i got to tell you about emma" he says,
happy
red cheeks
electricity in his hair.
"let's hear it" i say...

TRAMPLED

laura's a dominatrix

says her job

is to sit and walk on men and women

as heavy as possible there's no

sex, she says,

but that is sex, don't you see, i say...

"i trampled a woman so hard the other day

i think i broke one of her ribs",

well it's a wonderful life i say,

you got 20 bucks she says?

i hand it to her

she gives me a kiss

"still fucking the stripper down the hall?" i say

she winks, "don't tell mike."

shakes her haunch out the door

walks into her place

reggie's there with shiny eyes

got kicked out of the whorehouse

staying with mike and laura

she hates this

they argue constantly

all sorts of characters in and out of there

scene building up to no good timmy

asks laura to walk all over him

50 bucks says laura,

fuck you says timmy,

he shakes his head, he downs a scotch

he thinks of venice where he spent a summer

a long time ago

a delicate moment with his nephew

among the gondolas and the rabid intensity

he downs another scotch

laura's screaming at someone

mike's trapped somewhere in his head

i see emma from my gigantic sliding windows,

she walking in the sweltering heat high heels on

the cobblestone

GODDAMNIT, THERE SHE IS,

DON'T STOP YOU FUCKING WHORE

YOU BRILLIANT COLLECTION

OF MADNESS

YOU DAYGLO BITCH QUEEN, DON'T STOP!

THE MOST BEAUTIFUL THING

old bag of a caretaker

telling mike he's too late on rent

she got hump on back

gimp leg

ugliest human alive

spits out rage and disillusion

even the gang members

fear her

the gods tremble

timmy runs down hall

old bag gimpin' after him

sun going down

timmy has nephew

crazy talks and walks like

an adult

he freaky this kid

discusses life death the universe

waves his hand casually

puts smoke in his mouth

timmy slaps it out

then lights one of his own

tracy on corner

happy since bob in jail

she laughs with the neighbourhood

kids

she laughs at the sun

laura grim and wanton

eyes like laser beams

thighs like hercules

everything around her

urban madness

it grows

it ferments and follows

beer vendor on corner

unhappy and dead

guy behind counter face scarred

beyond recognition

eyes twisted

mouth not where it should be

something about a beating

dark people, dark thoughts

people turn away when they see him

mike and laura engage him in conversation

he gentle this monster

he kind and generous

i'm with him right now

small apartment he's got a beer in hand

he speaks i look at his face,

i listen intently,

i look

he's beautiful

i'm happy....

THE NIGHT IS ALIVE

reggie and timmy play
chess in central park,
both wired and hazy
tired and mournful,
but alive in fire and love,
shark slicing through water,
junkie laughing but sad,
cab-driver lost in negative zone,
rabid loon drowning in waste,
mother angry,
children blissful in ignorance,
what day is it, says timmy...

ain't no day, says reggie, make your move,
people gather,
native guy lights a smoke,
you should have moved your rook
he says to timmy,
yeah says timmy,

oh yeah...

someone sparks a joint
timmy he losing,
he an intellectual but reggie
from the streets man,
instincts riding high,
all sinew and energy and purpose,
there's a cat up a tree
eyeing a bird on a branch,
old man sits beside reggie,
they shake the hippie shake
up and over through gas-lit
back alleys
and the deadly sun overhead...

beautiful day, isn't it? says
one guy to another while reggie
makes his move,
timmy's nephew is there
he sitting on the grass
hand on chin

thinkin' deep thoughts,

i tell ya, this kid freaky...

mike shows up

eyes shiny with crack

laura happy dark cloud all around her

it's an afternoon in the core area of peg zero

time non-existent

they gathering their strength

for when sun-go-down,

when the vampires come out

and the children sleep,

the old timers drunk and tired,

street gangs sharpening their stilettos,

emma spreading her dark shadow,

timmy concedes game,

let's go says reggie,

where to? says timmy,

they all laugh,

get up,

start moving,

the night is here...

CINDY MAKES HER MARK

"you fucking asshole!" screams laura,
"i come home to THIS?"

mike laying there naked on his stomach
the words 'i love you' etched on his ass
in a feminine scrawl,
"i told you" he says, "i told you..."

laura screams at the top of her lungs,
she says nothing,
just screams,
like her suffering is paramount,
like the world trade centre was an illusion,
like children don't starve to death,
like babies don't get raped,
like terminal disease is a lie,
like the world isn't sinking
inch by inch flushed down the can
with random precision...

**"WAS IT CINDY THAT FUCKING BITCH,
WAS IT?"**
she slaps him,
he returns the favour,
she storms out of the apartment,
comes walking into mine...

she got a black mini-skirt
high heels
crying on my couch,
smoking cigarettes
blue smoke forming patterns
"he can't stand the fact i'm hooking" she says,
"but i'm doing it for us..."

she's got nice big thighs
porcelain white
legs crossed one shoe dangling from heel,
i look at the legs,
i smile,
she's crying and miserable,

i feel like laughing but instead i
light a joint and pass it to her...

she takes it...
LIKE NOTHING, LIKE HELL

you can only live one way,
your way,
everything else is bunk...

is that right? says timmy...

fucking ay, says his nephew,
as he reaches for the cigarettes...

watch your mouth, says timmy,
and don't even think about it...

PEG ZERO GHETTO WALK

cruising down ellice,

reggie collecting drug money,

pawn shops on every corner,

laundromat stinkin' and ugly,

-25 outside, snow blinding bright

reggie he talking with street punk

doing laundry living normal and clean

he tall and wiry and insane and precise

old lady doing laundry counting pennies

ragged clothes cursing in foreign language

reggie short on his take this week in trouble

he sees old lady arguing with owner no money

walks over pays for her laundry she afraid but

not for long

he walks her home carries laundry bags right

up to her apartment

has tea they talk and smoke cigarettes

apartment small but very clean

she from portugal he from barbados they
together in peg zero thirty years apart
the wind howling through the streets,
the snow piled high on every corner,
he alive,
she alive,
late on rent,
late on drug money
ain't it a kick?

YESTERDAY

mike leaning on post

outside public library

timmy inside doing his thing

"mike" says reggie,

"yeah?"

"gimme a light."

he inhales smoke burned-out eyes,

bob approaches

tracy hanging

on arm

they're laughing

they're happy

he pinches her ass

she kisses him

the sun is overhead

mike smiles blows out smoke

bob gives him the hippie handshake

waves him over to the corner

"i got it" says bob

puts tinfoil in mike's hand

"this is broad daylight buddy" says mike

"no worries"

"you'd better watch it, you're gonna

get popped one day"

"not a chance"

tracy comes running over

jumps on bob

they kissing young and wild

moving forward mike follows

then reggie

down the street lighting cigs., shooting the shit

through the concrete, the broken bottles

and car exhaust

"where's laura?" says tracy

"let me tell you" says mike...

STREET-FEST

she doesn't even feel it...

he penetrates

she thinks about her new toaster

legs spread like an atom bomb

she arches her hips

he strokes madly,

like fury and vengeance

he fucking her angry and desperate

she looks at the ceiling

counts the cracks

he's in the red zone

drop of sweat lands on her forehead

he starts to slow

making noises like dying animal

she thinks of her kids

of the roaches in her apartment

of her grandmother on the reserve

he slowly picks up the pace

their bellies flopping against each other
her groans deserving the oscar
she feels like laughing
she thinks of reggie's eyes
he gets a cramp in his left calf
trying to hide it body
tilting to one side
what the hell she thinks
he's howling like a banshee
she feels absolutely nothing
then it's over...

"you still have twenty minutes" she says
"i thought we might talk..."
"no talking allowed"
"what's your name?"
"destiny...what the fuck's the difference?"

at that precise moment i walk the downtown
streets
with laura,
there's a festival street blocked off

goes on for blocks and blocks

gigantic stages set up at each end

bands playing their blues

there are jugglers,

buskers

street vendors

face painters

fire walkers

cops everywhere

bumping into one every ten minutes

thousands of people walking

back and forth

abundant with life

color electricity blue sky crying

"weren't we supposed to meet them here?" says

laura

"yeah"

we hit the alleys,

pour some more southern comfort in our cups...

destiny on all fours

he slamming her violent

pulling hair,

pulling

ripping

clawing

banging everything in the world he detests

sounds of the festival echoing through

the streets

she screaming feeling the violence

once again

a smile forms on her lips

she pictures a bear in the woods

he's fucking her

she's laughing

he's fucking her

she's screaming...

mike and reggie

lost in the festival they trippin'

dancing through the urban landscape

mike drunk

reggie shiny-eyed bare-chested

raging at the world

the beautiful women of peg zero

passing by in jean shorts

and tank tops tanned bodies

in the madness circling like

vultures

mike stops one they start the dance

she got V.O. and coke

tall and slender

cool and desperate

reggie selling crack to teenagers

shaking hands with the followers

bum on street playing a flute

reggie drops twenty in his hat

they move to a back alley

as me and laura move to another...

she got arms around me

we're dancing in the street

40 degrees out here

sweat pouring down thousands

of bodies

sweat shining on laura's pearl-white skin

she got black mini-skirt

army boots

purple lipstick

instincts of a killer

she caressing the sweat on my face

my hands slide down her thighs

"let's smoke a joint" she says...

reggie he hangin'

mike beside him

they laughing and chillin'

cops two steps away

reggie he knows this

he likes it

likes the fear

only way to live man

kids playing hopscotch

reggie joins them

mike takes shot of whiskey

sun beating down without mercy

voices! music! lights!

they take a seat on the curb

watch the world go by...

destiny talking with madame
smoking cigarettes
talking gently under the air-conditioning
upstairs three guys fucking
she sees timmy's nephew walk by
smoking a cigarette
waving hands in the air
"that kid's freaky" says madame
"yeah" says destiny
she pours a whiskey
lights another smoke
"this festival is good for us" says madame
"yeah, great...shall we?"

sun going down
laura arguing with some scruff
owes her money
denies it
she insists
he denies it

i'm bored with entire game
thinkin' of venus and jupiter and
the crack of my ass
i take laura's arm direct her
in other direction
she screaming at scruff,
"you don't want me on your back asshole!"
we move through the enormous crowd
arm in arm like lovers
sweat cooling on our skin
southern comfort down our throats
"where the fuck are those guys?" she says...

trio of lesbians befriend us
laura excited handing out smokes
all three dead ugly
all three pleasant and happy
we're at the stage
sea of bodies and faces
reggae band grooving
jamming like the grateful dead
girl in bikini top and cut-offs smiles

i catch her eye

we're both doing the reggae hop

big gorilla approaches puts arm around her

i quickly turn to laura

rub her back

she winks

touches my ass

lesbians all around us

i spot a face in the insanity,

feel a chill,

"is that emma?" i say

laura freezes,

we hold hands...

mike and reggie sit in courtyard

surrounded by tables and chairs and lanterns

large water fountain in middle

air canada building to the right

all concrete and glass

moon up in dark sky

drinking beer smoking cigarettes

smell of hot-dogs and cheeseburgers all around
them
"it's a good life" says mike
"me thinkin'" says reggie "me thinkin'"...

"so do you have your rent for this month?"
says laura
"shhhhh, none of that shit tonight, look around
you"
we're sitting on a bench
festival keeps moving
families gone home
the rowdies are out
still beautiful and peaceful
everybody having a motherfucking ball
everybody enjoying the respite
everyone drunk and happy
even the cops are laughing
"look" says laura
i look,
we hold each other
we're smiling

she takes a shot of southern

"will you lookit that" i grin...

man tied to bed spread-eagled on his back

destiny trampling his body like an air cushion

he groaning in pain

she jumps on his ribs

she lights a cigarette

stomps on his cock

pounds his guts repeatedly

her daughter at home watching television

destiny thinks of david cronenberg

she thinks of homer simpson

and mordecai richler

man on floor she jumps on chest from bed

does it ten times in a row

time up...

mike and reggie leave the courtyard

five minutes later me and laura

sit in their chairs

"mike's in big shit" says laura

there's a fire-eater by the fountain
guy i know
bald head fringe living
he waves me over
lights a joint
we shoot the shit
tells me 80 thousand people are here
surprised from the lack of violence
it is peg zero after all
i shake his hand
move back to laura
never seen her so happy and alive
hasn't touched the crack pipe tonight
always told her to stay away from powder
family
she looks at me
she wants something
puts her feet on my lap,
"laura" i say...

early morning
we're at the river

no one around

sun just starting

skyline in the horizon

last of the southern

last cigarette

we're drunk-tired

we kiss

we kiss some more

i pull away

feeling guilty about mike

feeling squeamish about all the cocks inside her

she's angry

she understands

she kisses me on the cheek,

one last drink...

girl leans against window ass out

mike's ramming from behind

sun going up

she's sixteen

reggie with eighteen year old in living room

coke on the table

half empty beer on the floor

ashtray overflowing

reggie thinks of love

mike thinks of a bicycle he had as a kid

purple with funky handlebars

young girl leaves building

crosses paths with destiny on her way home

destiny sits in central park

lights a smoke

looks at the sun

mike stretches out alone

reggie gone with companion

echoes of festival in mike's head

he lights a smoke

laughs

key rattles, door opens,

laura walks in...

TALES FROM THE FROZEN CITY

-29 timmy and nephew
huddle in doorway then
move on,
wind tearing at their bones
timmy sucking on cigarette
hands in pockets
moving down sargent street
kennedy then ellice
even hookers indoors
even junkies and
politicians and
the wild moose of the northern plains,
they find a diner
hot coffee and bran muffins
timmy's nephew sits on bench
legs dangling off the edge
long-haired indian in corner

looks out window

sips on orange juice

lights a smoke,

fat man he tired and hungry

has notepad in front of him

pauses,

jots a few lines,

swallows coffee,

waitress young and pretty

annoyed by the banal and the obvious

she thinkin' of cory in her geography class

with his slender build

long sideburns,

timmy holds on to coffee mug

he terrified and righteous

bead of sweat down temple

nephew smiling at indian

waves his hand confident and assured

"what are we going to do?" says timmy

nephew shrugs his shoulders,

"what the fuck are we going to do?" says

timmy...

DOG DAY AND NIGHT

tracy walks down alley

radio in pocket she lifted

from party

last night on her way to pawn shop

she shakin' the junky chills

need a hit

need a fix

crow flies overhead

dog barks down the street

she thinks of her children for a moment,

just for a moment,

then keeps moving...

TRACY PLAYS GUITAR

playing guitar noise in the hallway

people be running up and down

she strums the jazz,

something from chet baker

all inside peaceful and sad

outside broken bottles

drunken shouts

"it can't be like this" she says quietly "it can't

be"

plays the a minor

then the f

and the g

soft sounds

small changes in the air,

she hears the horn

the entire melody,

there's a black man brushing the drums

another tapping the bass

gently

chet's voice reeling in the sky

she improvises

chet smiles

he throws in a riff,

the phone rings goddamit

she pauses,

the insanity outside continues,

the phone keeps ringing

chet's waving goodbye

black guy sparking reefer

she looks at the crack pipe

all gone

all distant and confused,

she picks up the phone,

"hello"

"hello, tracy skinner?"

"yeah"

"this is social assistance calling we-"

it all goes down from there...

PARTY IN 1607

there's a party in 1607
reggie he checking it out
kicking back pipe in hand
there be reefer going around
20 scattered people gettin' drunk
and high wasted nights in the casba
reggie he talkin' to young pretty girl,
pretty girl she eyein' the tall native guy
reggie by window now,
couple cool joes shoot the shit
he speaking his best barbados accent,
argument in corner
blood on the floor,
it ain't nothing he says,
ain't nothing at all...

hip hop in background
reggie wishing for jazz
but the ladies they all around man,

they slick and whiskey young,

more arguments,

some laugh,

some feel the fear,

reggie collecting money for the drug parade

they huddle by the table,

they light the pipe like it's a token to the gods,

reggie waves in a young thing of 19 or 20

she already livin' on pluto

among the clouds and the gastown memories,

glassy eyes she looks up,

reggie smiles,

it begins now...

another party in 1603

reggie there now

white boys from middle-class

slumming it for the thrill

reggie he bored

reggie he tired

white girls looking good

everybody flat and humorless

things too easy he thinkin',
the whiskey comes out
then the grass and the coke
reggie getting along now
entire room in synch,
for awhile,
just awhile,
then the first argument,
it begins now...

we're at my place,
1803,
few buddies sitting around
we got the whiskey and the grass
reggie talks to me continuously,
"man" he says "you're place is an island in all
this shit",
"reggie, reggie" i say
"me thinkin', me thinkin'"
i got the sex-pistols on the ghetto
raunchy and anti-everything,
couple women by window

they loving the view,

i'm wondering about their legs,

their eyelashes,

the color of their underwear,

"pretty amazing view" she says,

i smile and introduce her to reggie,

it begins now...

THE FIRST DROPS OF RAIN HIT THE PAVEMENT

"you know, in italy there are gypsies
everywhere, pulling scams on everyone..." i say

"well ain't that nice" says native guy on corner,
we shake hands, move on,
in central park mike sits on grass
with laura
lazy day in the shade
kids running around
invulnerable
annoying
and
beautiful,
mike and laura they talking
about things,
money
drugs

all of those good times

laura promises to quit hooking

soon,

soon she says,

mike's smiling

he caressing her face

they're kissing like teenagers

wrestling on the grass

looking at the clouds,

laura lights a joint

two weeks

without the crack they're

feeling better,

they're laughing under the sun

playing basketball with the neighborhood

kids,

other side of park

they see reggie,

he gliding his way towards them,

they shake hands,

"wanna party tonight?" he says,

shows them the tinfoil,

laura and mike look at each other,

they look around, up above

it's clouding over

then laura's eyes light up,

"let's go" she says,

the first drops of rain hit the pavement...

LAURA ON ALL FOURS

some guy banging her from behind

she fucking him for crack

four or five people in room

all high

all drunk

pills

powder

and grass

laura in the middle of the room

she howling

that mother driving her

with violence

each stroke more vicious than the next

people smiling

sweating

one other woman has middle finger

in laura's mouth

laura sucking

groovin' and diggin' it

things get silent

hypnotic

everyone in a trance

laura thinks very briefly

of her dead father

that fucker drives her one last time

then it's over...

they applaud

laura laughing on the outside

inside torn and shattered

they hand her the pipe

she inhales deeply

has a toke and a

beer

some bullshit conversation,

"more" she says pointing

to the pipe...

he gestures towards the middle of the room...

she lays down and spreads her legs...

ME THINKIN', MAN, ME THINKIN'

on a park bench
surrounded by cement
and car exhaust
reggie lights a smoke,
sits back...
"i want to be better man, me always thinkin'"
he says...
"i hear ya reggie" i say, "don't worry things
will pick up"...

he pauses just to look at the sun,
eyes tired and knowing,
you can see barbados in those eyes,
there be light, beauty and sadness,
"man, that fucker kicked me out of the
whorehouse,
me stayin' with a friend just over there..."

he waves a hand,
it falls to his side in defeat,
world closing in
world distant and uncaring
goo goo doll electric
on fire insane
rabid sensation running mad
running stillness down the back alleys,
"that laura" says reggie "she fucking crazy,
crazy bitch...she do
mike no good, you know that?"...

sun going down
scattered shadows paint the streets
reggie got eyes to the ground
lean body in trouble
i put my hand on his shoulder
flip him a ten
he smiles but not really
starts walking away full of street and attitude
i watch that body glide through
the neon and the gasoline

the rusted sewer mains

a cat bolts right by me,

i get up,

light a smoke,

the theatre is letting out

couples walk by hand in hand,

a line-up begins to form,

next act at 9:30 ladies and gentlemen,

enjoy the show...

CROCODILE BEER

mike runs into tracy

on the corner of broadway and osborne,

"this ain't no L.A. scene" she says,

she begging for money

she broke and hungry

wants a fix

mike looks at her tiny beautiful body

face in pain

face looking ugly and old

"tracy, come with me" he says,

she follows,

unable to do anything else

she follows...

THREE DAYS TO CHRISTMAS

three days to christmas
laura stands in line at
food bank
hooker money all gone
two days without eating
she jonesin' for a hit
stomach screaming for food
mind begging for answers
guy behind her shuffles his feet
girl up ahead spits on the sidewalk
church on the corner plays christmas carols
it begins to snow...
temperature rises...
laura lights a smoke...

line gets smaller
old chinese lady smiles in the wind

pushes shopping cart up a snow bank

laura takes one last puff

her hair white from snow tears slide down her

cheek...

EVERYTHING ALRIGHT

on corner of qu'appelle street and carlton

four story apartment full of fringe living

bob sits on floor stares out window

tracy beside him lights a joint

snow coming down like a blanket

"it's alright" he says,

"are you sure?"

"everything's alright"

he takes the joint

blows out perfect smoke circles

that rise to the ceiling,

bug crawls across the floor,

bob takes tracy's hand and squeezes

he kisses her lightly,

they hold each other

pennies in their pockets

snow outside the window...

STREETLIGHTS AND HANGOVERS

my place just down the street from qu'apelle
corner of cumberland and carlton
facing central park size of a soccer field
dotted with large trees and park benches
streetlights and hangovers
it's summer...

night so hot brain screams like fire
i'm in the park
starry sky high-rise on either side of me
church on the corner
old folk home on next
night is silent but echoes of danger always
present
a whistle in the distance
a shout from a window
a beer bottle smashing on the cement

core area of peg zero on a tuesday night

i think of emma

always emma with her stiletto heels

and wiry grin

all electricity and motion

death beauty and desperation

emma

always

and

forever

the footsteps come up behind me like a train

wreck...

FRIDAY NIGHT

mike just finished graveyard shift

approaching central park

sun up blinding,

old asian men practice tai-chi,

a bum down the street shakes off his hangover,

mike breathes the cool morning air

feeling good,

lights smoke hand shaking,

he laughs

tries to stop it,

hand shaking

ain't nothing man,

just got paid,

pocket full of change,

he thinkin' friday night man,

friday night...

FAMILY

destiny in a mall at the food court

son with her

small boy of eight

just looking for food and gasoline

line-up hungry bastards

fifty cent coffee and egg muffins

young guy missing ear stands behind destiny

he smiles at her son

kid turns away uninterested,

"mommy" he says 'mommy"

"yeah.."

they eat and move on,

sitting on park bench she laughing

son laughing toy airplane in hand

cars fly by

action lights and sound

destiny and son aware only of each other

she tickles him

bus pulls up

ragged guy gets off
then old lady
a couple of teenagers
slightly bent over native guy
approaches them,
"there's uncle" says destiny
kid excited
he screaming wild
uncle lifts him and spins around
while bum begs for pennies in front
of corner store,
"i'll pick him up tomorrow afternoon" says
destiny
"listen, sorry about last time i..."
"no drinking around the kid"
she walks away lights a smoke
walks down sargent
then ellice
jean shorts hugging ass-cheeks like bowling
balls
she thinks about her brother
her son

her grandmother up north
sex
french fries and the war on terrorism,
takes a drag butts her smoke
there's a bar on the corner of ellice and
kennedy
couple tough guys in front shootin' the shit
she walks by them through the front door
bartender handsome and tough
she orders a scotch looks around cigarette in
mouth
spots a familiar face and approaches,
i watch her long black curls bouncing towards
me
"how are ya?" she says,
she sits beside me,
i take a sip of rye and lose myself in her
thighs...

TAI CHI IN THE PARK

bob and tracy lay in bed

sunday afternoon they've been here all day

sun comes through blinds in shafts

bob gentle and kind to her

tracy feeling happy

they share a joint

fucking around in the dim light

bullshitting like everything's

wildfire running through your backyard

purple haze in the grim sun

chills at the local tavern...

both on welfare but bob got job lined up

cleaning buses 13 bucks an hour

tracy wants to stay home and play guitar

"it's okay" says bob "i'll take care of things"...

bob in elevator 6 am.

coming from mike's place on the 18th

young native woman walks in on the 9th

smelling like booze she starts talkin'

"just got in a fight with my old man"

"yeah?"

"does my eye look bruised?"

"don't think so"

"got any pot?"

bob looks down at the floor,

"what's that?"

"got any pot?"

"no"

"how about smokes, any smokes i can bum?"

elevator stops on 2nd parking level,

albanian fellow walks in nods at bob

starts yelling at woman

woman gives it back

at ground level bob shoves guy to the side

moves out the door through the hallway

into the convenience store,

arab fellow sits behind counter

nervous eyes flecks of grey in his moustache,

"pack of du mauriers" says bob

"how are you?"
"good"
"you sure?"
they shake hands
sun coming up
bob lights smoke
tai chi in the park
old asian fellows gathering the energy
spreading it out through the grey and blue
bob sits on bench smokes cig,
the old men continue
waving in and out over under
bob's eyes junky bloodshot
"yeah" he shouts "YEAH!",
couple university students shuffle by
bob smiles, he smiles, keep walking he gestures,
"fucking freak" says one student to the other,
"hey, watch your mouth...going to the gig
tonight?"
"got a paper on representative lit due...maybe"
"we're gonna be late"
"just a fifteen minute jog to campus, c'mon",

they leave the park running,

bob sees them fade behind an old elm tree,

"fucking students" he says "faggots",

cracks his last beer

stares into the sun

fully confident in his assumption of himself

he laughs

closes his eyes

remembers nothing more

lit cigarette falls on his chest burning

in the cool chill morning...

POETRY HELL

timmy sits with mike beer in
front of him
bookstore cafe timmy got the tao
from lao tze
mike fighting a hangover
the trendy all around seems
someone doing a reading later
stage set up chubby girl
with john lennon glasses
squabbles over stage lighting
mike with dirty jeans
timmy got greasy hair
nervous smile
through window he sees his nephew
group of kids around him
he holding court like buddha
his flunkies hanging on every word,
"that's one strange kid" says mike
"you're telling me?" says timmy,

poet starts reading

words fly through the air

completely irrelevant and insulting

"let's go" says mike

timmy gets up, checks his pockets

"where we goin'?" he says

"the fuck away from here" says mike...

AFTER ALL

old fucking hag of a caretaker

roams the hallways

can't get nothin' by her

hump on back greasy ugly

gimp leg surrenders nothing

"what you doin'?" she tells mike

he sits there and explains like he figures

he has to,

back in his apartment laura talks

about her mother,

bob takes a puff,

albanian guy there he drinking like it's

the end of the world,

he drinking man

he drinking,

peg zero all around them

-19 outside,

central park like an ice-rink,

church on the corner dead silent

everything frozen mad and laughing

there's this busker does his thing on

the corner of portage and hargrave

plays the flute drunken lousy

always smilin'

always happy

i walk by him on a hot saturday afternoon

we shake hands i sit and listen

to the flute echo through the buildings

the street corners

the lost business men

the indians alive and hungry

all the fucked up ideas and wandering

bouncing from this corner to that

from one side of peg zero to the next,

"gimme a drink" he says "gimme a drink"...

SHOOTING HOOPS IN THE MOONLIGHT

reggie at bus-stop he running

the drugs man

smokes more than he sells

owes money to everyone

walks the streets with a buck-fifty

in his pocket

church on corner tall beautiful spirals

he sits on steps lights a bowl

afternoon in central park

black kids shooting hoops

white kids there as well

chinese fellow with girlfriend they

kissing in the sunlight

here comes laura...

she dark like an atom bomb

white skin glows with addiction

takes a seat lights a smoke

then pauses,

fucking hot summer day

laura in black

black only - soccer ball comes her way

kid gestures moves towards her

she tickles him laughing

he got snotball on upper lip

"you're pretty" he says

"i know" she laughs

reggie spots her they together now...

passing the crack pipe like a trophy

"where's mike?" he says

"hmmm" she muses

reggie talkin' 'bout being broke

got no money

got no home

he lousy drug dealer

she lousy drug addict

"my mother's crazy" she says

"who ain't, me thinkin' man, me thinkin'"

he's asking for money now

laura explodes as she will

she slaps his face over and over

reggie he's taking it from side to side

he taking it cool like the barbados

central park moves on as always

through the desperate bizarre hangovers of peg

zero

down the core area and the cobblestone of paris

the frozen landscape of the indian reserves

the isolation of the canadian prairies

same thing over and over

he cool man,

reggie cool...

ON THE JUKE

rock and roll on the jukebox

the stones, screamin' blue messiahs,

and elvis costello

"what about the butthole surfers?" says mike

music loud crazy

brain gone wild

scattered people hangin' out

mike keeps talking in my ear

yeah, oh yeah, i say,

couple of girls they drinking gin

so automatic man, so automatic

they talking to me

me talking to them

mike in my ear again lips touching my cheek

"let me show you something" he says

poster on wall of hunter s. thomson

well, i'm thinkin', well well

mike puts hand on my ass smiles

he looking at me with deep sorrow eyes

ain't no way mike i say, ain't no way,

his hand hovers over my crotch fading smile

one more move, i say, one more move our

friendship

is over,

sorry sorry

i put my arm around him,

no problem buddy

and move away...

east indian girl by window

i like her accent

we talking and smoking

marijuana everywhere

tight t-shirt big tits the gods are calling

someone's got a guitar singing

hippie songs from the waste zone,

time to go i figure,

i see mike

he lookin' sad and distant

laura walks in i pass her on way out

down the hallway walk into my place

cd's scattered in front of huge windows

facing the city skyline and the ghetto down

below

i put on the replacements...

i light a joint...

pour a rye and 7...

i think about emma

emma

always

and

forever...

DOMINATRIX ON MY COUCH

laura telling me mike's sucking cock for money
"don't care laura" i say "his mouth, his life"
never figured mike was into this shit
don't give a damn i repeat, don't give a damn
laura on my couch in full dominatrix gear
time to work she's saying
cigarette in her fingers
red pumps dangling
torn fishnet a visual assault
vampire bites tattooed on her neck
pushing at my jeans
i'm helping her with outfit
thick cord around her neck
i'm pulling
tighter, she says, tighter
face turning blue
this is very strange i'm thinkin'

she laying on my couch

one porcelain thigh reaching for the ceiling

pumps off she's asking me to kiss her feet

"what the fuck for?" i say

telling me she sad and lonely

lost and gray

"i love mike" she says

"i can see that" i say have a beer

have a shot for the fuck of it

for the sheer absurdity and total loss

she directs that rage of hers at me for the first

time

an ashtray flies by my head

for the first time,

for the last time...

CANDY ASS

shitty job flippin' burgers
at corner diner
timmy cursing out loud 3rd day
on the job,
nephew at the middle booth
he smilin' legs dangling at the edge
timmy curses again
boss kind of cool fat guy from greece he
encourages timmy,
don't worry, he says, no worries he thinking
of old girlfriend back home on the sand
and in the water,
timmy looks at nephew
kid taunting him flashing teeth
lunch time...

he sits with nephew talking about moupassant
cold ideas in the hot car exhaust afternoon
woman walks by shaking haunch

nephew muses

i need a drink says timmy

me too says nephew

off goes the apron 3rd day on the job,

last day...

THE GROOVE

things crumbling for reggie

drug dealer cans his ass

he doing anything for a buck

bob with him tired of work

tired of 9 to 5 expectations

they breaking into apartments now

broken down core area dwellings

nothing to steal 'cept five dollar ghetto blasters

false teeth on the dresser and

g. i. joe with the kung-fu grip

tracy sinking into powder land

strumming jazz guitar barefoot

in the hazy desert broken beer bottles

on the pavement

car horns in the distance reggie

running through parking lot

bob ahead of him they laughing

they got a radio, 50 bucks and an old

rambo movie

gray old cat out of nowhere runs

reggie down he kicks it reaching for the sky

crazy thing does a beautiful arc

hits the ground keeps running

it's a blast

it's an epiphany

life's a gas

sun coming up laura pours tea

mike's draped over the couch

laura says something wiry grin

they laugh

they shaking with it feeling the groove

curled up by the windows facing central park

horizon in the distance

old fellow pissing on a tree it's a good day

ain't no better

ain't no way...

LAURA AND REGGIE

young guy too much cock in his walk

bob and tracy's neighbor

sleeves cut off he got a mullet

rides a ten speed down the streets

tracy got a shine for him

they talk like it ain't worth it

he walks away her eyes follow

another coffee and a cigarette

a pipeful of hash

a blast of crack,

on the corner of balmoral and sargent kid

riding a bike shouting at the sidewalk,

down by old market square the shops are lit up

and the artists argue,

reggie on park bench puffing smoke

drinking coca cola laura beside him

she looking out

she takes his hands

her mouth closes around his

she rubbing his crotch

hold it he says

points to an old lady walking by

a young barefoot couple in fringes

they kiss again feeling guilty

feeling sad

feeling right...

UNDER THE SHADOWS

mike's at party on langside and ellice
always a dirty trip on this street broken-down
fences small yards huge trees casting shadows
on the sidewalk,
few native gang members hanging out in
kitchen he sits with them passing crack
back and forth hot
gang chicks hangin' tough long table covered in
beer bottles
"what's your name?" says one
"mike, here, have a smoke"
bags under eyes he smiles got good looks still on
the edge of everything
girl on his lap bouncing
guy with long ponytail puts on iron maiden
large native fellow in corner showing his latest
artwork to a couple young women painting of a
long winding river at dusk indian chief in the
sky

"cool" they're saying "right on baby" tits
bouncing halter-tops dark homemade tattoos
on shoulders hands forearms
one has bad rendition of eagle just above right
breast
mike's long long curls moving side to side finds
native artist
both diggin' the other right off working
the women mike ends up
in washroom sloppy blow job on dirty floor
artist loud crazy wild raunchy women dig him
tension with some of the boys
sawed-off shotgun in bedroom on small table
mike sees it all night long through slightly ajar
door gives him the fucking creeps
shows artist doesn't give a shit,
"i'm from pukatawagan man" he says "that
ain't nothing..."

party spills outside yard packed already two
different fights

angry laughter everywhere artist and mike
getting into it
with a group of gang-bangers artist throws a
kick
gang moves in mike and artist are down
knees and kicks are everywhere
somehow artist slips out he already running
down the street group follows few remain keep
kicking mike
party goes on as always he grabs a foot pushes
up
punk goes flying he grabs broken fence post
other punk's head
snaps forward then backward
now he's running man
the night is drunk few guys behind him they're
cutting in and out of yards dog barking
lights going on guys get tired
mike keeps moving then stops...

ribs are sore he sits in park hot summer night

clothes stuck to his body sweat running down

his

face blood on his lips

but okay he's thinking

okay

still got drugs in his pocket

fridge full of beer at home

almost dawn

line of red and orange on the horizon

sky beginning to turn a pale blue

he follows his feet stumbles home tired of more

than he can remember...

LATE NIGHT ENDING

"where were you last night?" says laura from
the washroom down the hall,
"at a party on langside" says mike
looking through fridge finds an O.V. hands
shaking
he alright moonlight in the window,
moon high above central park everything
shakes
under the neon cigarette lit bottle tipped
forwards
laura comes out of the washroom down the hall
enters room in black underwear pierced
nipples
wet hair trailing down her back,
hair jet-black and thick like the devil's she
smiles
mike puts his arm around her soft kisses
in the neon moonlight everything shakes....

DESTINY GOES FOR A DRIVE

destiny waits on street corner maryland and
sargent
one car goes by then nothing all silent...
3 am she waits for that bastard chain smoking
under burned-out streetlight
ambulance flies by lights flash orange
faint sound of music down the street heavy bass
got her heels tapping
lightly leather jacket covers her ass tight jeans
legs shifting left to right
looks straight up into the sky crescent moon
directly above city skyline seems on fire
red and yellow almost blinding
destiny starts singing childhood song
softly at the moon
car pulls up,
"motherfucker" says destiny,

"sorry girl, get in"

back seat full three big native boys pot smoke

clouds the view her brother in driver's seat tells

buddy in passenger,

"get the fuck in back man, that's my sister's

seat"

she beside him they're moving rip-speed

into the west-end hangover guaranteed

beer comes from the back seat

she takes it feeling fucked-up-happy

pills are popped rock and roll on the radio

"dez got kicked out of his apartment" says

brother,

"no shit?" says destiny,

"gets home from an all-nighter lock's changed

with all his shit inside"

"crazy shit man"

boys in back seat laughing getting rowdy,

"reggie's moving the crack now in the core"

says destiny,

"reggie? he's too happy-go-lucky man, people

are gonna fuck his ass, what happened to bob?"

"got popped"

"no shit man?"

"he was ratted out"

"no doubt, that's the only way it

happens...know who?"

"no, too many people involved, he supplied the

whole fucking neighborhood"

"bob was cool man"

"he was an asshole, these pills are kicking in,

let's get the fuck there already!"

everybody roars almost in unison car moves

forward group of punks running down the

street another group in pursuit car almost hits

them they scream

move out of way keep moving full-speed

to nowhere nothing doing man destiny

lights cigarette blood pumping she getting

angry

sounds like dirty water to me she's thinking,

out for a good time with a vengeance they

come up the driveway approach the house

large crowd in the front yard

motorhead blaring cases of beer stale cigarettes

violence in the air

young guy screaming "fuck the moon, fuck the

moon!"

couple leaning on fence both got bandannas

there are large trees everywhere

she clenches her fist as the car gets nearer

monkeys in the back getting louder

brother shuts off engine

they get out car doors slam

she looks up at the sky

moon no longer visible she gulps her beer

one step after the other...

TWO KIDS LAUGHING

tracy talking with mullet-head he got cut-off
sleeves
black sweats smoking cigarettes drinking beer
out
of coffee mug hot afternoon in the park by the
river
he's passing her a joint telling her,
"i was in jail three different times"
"how long? i mean, for what?"
"few months each time, just small bullshit
stuff"
"how was it?"
"it was awesome, i know everybody in there, as
long as you're not a pussy, you're alright"
she curls up to him blood boiling needs a fix
man
he's got money they share a beer
back in his apartment they're doing rock
she's smiling blowing kisses thinking

how much she hates this guy...

bob just two blocks down the street arguing
with
reggie he screaming,
"i told you no fucking violence man!"
"take it easy reggie, he'll be alright, here"
reggie looks at the money in bob's hands closes
his eyes,
endless blue beach crystal clear water as far as
the eye can see
black kids running up and down the golden
sand selling coconuts
a woman under a mango tree
a voice in the distance, "reggie you little
bastard..."
"you can keep that money man, don't be
coming around me either" says reggie
walks out door down stairs past young asian
woman in jean shorts
stops at the bottom
pause

walks right back up

knocks on the door,

"bob" he says "bob..."

tracy on her back mullet-head banging away

there's a train in the distance

thin stream of light coming through blinds

a flash in her brain of her children on the living

room floor laughing

she thinks of bob

goddamn him

an alarm clock goes off in the distant sunlight

cat on street corner makes you howl

tough shit baby,

it ain't happening...

PAUSE IN THE RIFF, GUITAR SOLO IN E

timmy looking at records in old pawn shop

dusty paperbacks on shelf spilling over the edge

all around the room there are records and

books and comic books

and old action toys from the seventies

his nephew got the bionic woman doll in his

hand staring at it intently

starts to whisper a song

owner comes round corner and smiles,

"what's up kid?"

timmy puts paperback in pocket grabs nephew

they hit the streets

"we're almost there" says timmy "few more

grabs and we're on our way"

nephew smiles lightly scratching his balls

large blond woman sees timmy from across the

street

starts moving towards him

"jesus" says nephew,

they start moving she screaming, "where's my

money faggot! where's my, uhh, uhhg, where's

my money?"

they in back lane large woman moving like

lightning

they can't believe their eyes mounds of flesh

rippling

down the back alley,

nephew eyes wide with fear timmy urging him

on

"jesus!" he says "fucking hell!"

large woman close sucking serious air but

moving grease-lightning

trips on something feet in the air comes down

hard

timmy and nephew laughing get out of alley

scale a fence through a construction site

and they're off

laughing at their damn miserable luck

nephew says something brilliant timmy

pauses for a second, just for a second,

then it starts again...

LIKE LSD IN THE RAIN

reggie in with laura now

gray clouds moisture in the air

rain taking its sweet fucking time

she's on the couch looking out hoping it might

rain today

and always

he writing songs in the bedroom reggae tune

like acid trip,

"what we got?" he says from around the corner

"some pot, but that's it baby"

she scratches her ass and lights a smoke

black tights, purple toenails, purple shirt three

buttons undone,

joint is lit he takes it,

she fuming mad suddenly slaps him hard

joint flies out of his mouth

"nobody hits this nigger, bitch!

nobody!...where's that joint?"

they're kissing heavy by open windows rain
falling in rhythm
over the rooftops of peg zero
laura thinks of mike,
reggie sliding thin hand down her pants
she starts to moan...

EVEN THE WIND

once again behind bars bob

stares out window cold autumn chill

in for long haul this time

they won't forgive violence he thinks,

not violence,

cockroach crawls over toilet in filthy corner

toothbrush by mirror grim and distant

he looks at the trees in the distance moving in

the wind

barbwire fence seems a touch away

just a hop and a skip man, can't believe it he

says,

can't fucken believe it,

figure catches his eye fear grips his sphincter

dark shadow by fence looking up at him

wild hair in the wind she stands teeth clenched

insane smile,

it's me she says,

emma he says, resigned and finally defeated,

finally she says,

dark heels on the pavement car door slams shut

then she's gone...

alright says bob, it's okay,

tears down his cheeks even the wind says

nothing...

OUT OF NOWHERE

north entrance of central park there's a large
fountain,
kiddie park with pool, swings, jungle bars,
mike beside me on the swings
leaves turned golden under our boots,
"laura's with reggie man" he says
"figured...saw them together last week"
rain falling slowly like we got all the time in the
world
couple kids running past us
old jamaican lady one eye missing sitting
on a bench by fire hydrant
at other end of park timmy and nephew barely
visible walking away from us
"how do you feel man?" i say
"fucked up, but fuck'em"
hands shaking slightly he looks at the ground
fire truck out of nowhere sirens blasting
races down the street fades into the distance

all silent after the bomb we start laughing...
then it stops...

"fuck it" i say
"yeah, fuck it"

TWENTY BUCKS FOR A BLOW-JOB

almost all here tonight small pub they got

burgers and onion rings

reggie he laughing mike shaking his hand

tracy laughs lightly

laura singing punk-drunk

movement around the table reggie looks at

laura midnight smile she fucked-up way out

there on the corner

mike bites into fried carcass

"what a blast" he says,

"what a blast" says laura strokes his arm

they kiss, reggie he thinkin'

laura in the washroom now black lipstick

torn fishnets

army boots gone wild

she spins round and out the door

reggie he there,

"you ain't said it yet" he says,
"no, back off man"...then she smiles,
her eyes hold his as long as they want
then turn away ass bouncing,
"tonight, cool?" she sweet sugar kisses now
reggie under the gun he's a back door man,
back at the table tracy missing bob,
"he was a good man actually...i remember one
night..."
she scratches her nose and rubs her hands
small smile speaks volumes
she's wishing she could mention mullet-head,
says something else,
"what's that?" says mike,
she rubs his arm sad eyes he looks
back in full agreement...
eighties music small club on second floor
everyone in black man dance floor in steel cage
strobe lights going madness
reggie dancing with tracy
mike and laura in corner by transsexual kissing
bartender large bushy beard,

they in back alley now clear blue sky turning
purple
couple of goth guys got the crack pipe
going back and forth mike digging it
laura talkative when in good mood
stunning inside and out,
she takes a puff small smile
mike kisses her,
goth guy does as well,
his friend kisses her kneecaps,
electra-glide-down-subzero...

"LET'S GO OVER THERE" says reggie
music so loud tracy follows they know
bartender
talking over counter hands and elbows all
around them
bartender tilts head behind him,
back kitchen reggie trying to borrow money
bartender got no problem with it baseball cap
long ponytail

tracy looking in small broken mirror sees

reflection she's smiling,

"i'll bring it tomorrow" says reggie,

they do the hippie shake

tracy running like underage porn star

they're on the dance floor

then they're outside in back alley,

he pulls out the pipe,

she's grinning,

air turns blue,

homo walks by offers a blow job for twenty

bucks,

"fuck you" says reggie,

tracy throws rock in his direction,

"let's do it" she says,

"got nothing but time my girl"...

she sits up knees drawn arms around them,

he's on edge of bed smoking cigarette,

deadly space between them silence pitch black

unmoving moment,

even the air, the sky, the room, the world has
stopped,
there's a woman's sneaker in the corner,
an overflowing ashtray in the other,
there are tears in her eyes she lets them roll
sun coming up
red
blue
yellow and terrifying,
suddenly a scream outside the window
all violent
all wrong she thinks, all wrong,
the world shatters into crystal powder
he grabs the knapsack puts it on shoulder,
"mike..." says laura ..."i'm sorry, i'm so
sorry..." she says,
he smiles and walks out
down the hall right past my door
tv on girl's beside me eyes laughing
i flip the channel and tell her i love her...

WELCOME TO THE USA

jesus man, says timmy's nephew bus sliding

side to side on ice road

timmy hanging on full of people on it's way

to minneapolis some scared others

uninterested approaching american border

timmy's nervous he got package

hands it to nephew eyes wide open

here it comes says timmy,

nephew he thinkin' they should have stayed in

canada

bus driver got damn thing under control now

moving

in straight line to the good ol' USA,

they're going to fuck us good says nephew,

america my ass,

strange silence comes over bus passengers

feeling nervous and shitty,

timmy puts hand on nephew's shoulder

kid shittin' man, he got package

tucked under arm, wraps his hand tighter,

large black fellow from the back comes closer

building with lights and people in uniforms

coming right up man,

timmy and nephew at front window almost side

to side with driver,

there's a slight rustle in back, a movement of

things,

people restless maybe afraid

bus slows then comes to a halt,

jesus says nephew,

hold on kid, says timmy,

it's do or die...

EMMA STRUNK

deep deep in the middle of summer
so damn hot your skin peels off of you
there's a section of central park
at far edge closed off for
the old timers to play horseshoes,
small bench under thick green elm trees
always in the shade on this corner i light
a smoke couple old guys throwing metal
fully dressed in slacks and vests and moving
around
looking cool and breezy while i
sit on bench sweating ass off see reggie
approaching been long time,
he got dirty clothes and dreadlocks now,
seems wiry out of rhythm look in eyes tired and
distant
"laura's mom died man" he says,
i say nothing,

"died while fucking some bum from main

street"

"where's laura?" i say,

"don't know man, nobody knows..."

we're silent for a second,

"laura, she gone anyway man, laura gone long

time ago..."

light breeze hair in my face i do nothing

to stop it, goes back and forth over my skin

feels like a woman's touch,

"why'd you go with laura man, she was with

mike, no reason for what you did"

"it was love man, don't you see?"

"fuck you buddy"

"got any money?"

i walk away look back once

he's walking in other direction

like old man hunched and bent over,

i'm in my building down the hall i see

large man with waist-long hair moving into

mike's old place,

i open my door piece of paper under it

flies across the room,

grab it last warning from caretaker for

august's rent,

stand at windows facing north large flock

of birds fly in formation

their sounds echo through the buildings...

mike sits up naked on the edge of bed touches

her lightly

"amazing" he says,

she smiles confident and happy,

"don't know what i'm feeling" she says,

destiny rolls over and grabs a beer takes a sip

hands it to him

both feeling the room and the world outside the

window

she smiles

he does too

they stand against each other destiny a good

head taller

light from outside barely reaches them,

"i saw emma the other day" she says

"that's impossible" he says

"why?"

"she doesn't exist"...

her shoes tap tap the pavement

pirouette down the boulevard

i see her from my window while the birds fly

overhead

she hails a cab

she laughing,

she gone whiskey-wild,

glide easy manic the infinite blindness

she emma

always and

forever

cab driver lets her in a

chill runs down his spine,

no one laughs like they should...

Tony Nesca was born in Torino, Italy in 1965 and moved to Canada at the age of three. He was raised in Winnipeg but relocated back to Italy several times until finally settling in Winnipeg in 1980. He taught himself how to play guitar and formed an original rock band playing the local bars for several years. At the age of twenty-seven he traded his guitar for a Commodore 64 and started writing seriously. He has published six chapbooks of stories and poems (which he used to sell straight out of his knapsack at local dives and bookstores), six novels, four books of poetry, one short story collection, and has been an active contributor to the underground lit scene for fifteen years, being published in innumerable magazines both online and in print. He currently resides in Winnipeg.

Screamin' Skull Press
Cutting Edge
Spontaneous
Street-Writing
Novels, Stories, Poems
Tony Nesca
Nicole I. Nesca

www.ingramcontent.com/pod-product-compliance
Lightning Source LLC
Chambersburg PA
CBHW022204050726
47590CB00002B/632